CATRINA BROWN

Guess Who's CUMMIN?

I0592643

AN EROTIC TWIST

Catrina Brown

GUESS WHO'S CUMMIN?

Trixie Publications

557 Hoxie Avenue

Calumet City, Illinois 60409

To the best of said publisher's knowledge, this is an original manuscript and is the sole property of the author known as **CATRINA BROWN.**

Printed in the United States of America

ISBN: 978-0-692-09821-9

Printed by Ingram Sparks 2018

Acknowledgments

Catrina D. Brown, an African-American woman born and raised in the South East side of Chicago, without any degrees in English or Journalism and with no knowledge of or help in writing a book, has now written 3 books and is working on number 4. Google became her guide.

Giving honor to God for allowing me to pen another book and live, love and laugh.

To my sons Justin, Alonzo and Russell Jr., thank you for being my ROCKS!!!

To my Jade Alexis, Laura , Istosh and Johnny, this has been a rough year, save my place. I miss you all along with other family and friends.

My Jade Amena, I'm so in love with you.

To my county family, thank you for showing up and showing out. I really appreciate your love and support.

To my Brown family and friends, you all have been instrumental lessons in my life and I thank you.

GUESS WHO'S CUMMIN?

To my fans, new, old, positive or negative; thank you all for your loving support. It helps aid me on all levels in becoming the best I can be.

Thank you.
Sincerely
Catrina D. Brown

 *Blessings!!!!!!!!!!!!!!!!!!!!!*

Introduction

As I sit, looking at every day objects and shapes, my imagination begins to wander and explore the erotic possibilities. I began to see these things as sensual beings, discovering new ways to turn them into objects that stimulate the sexual, sensual inner freak in us all.

Being intimate physically is one thing; however, in your imagination, your mind is where foreplay truly begins and it can be explosive. Stimulating the mental is key to true eroticism.

Enjoy my erotic game, not knowing where I'm "cummin" from, with an open mind, quiet intimate setting and your favorite glass of wine, cocktail or cup of tea.

Guess Who's CUMMIN?

AN EROTIC TWIST

Catrina Brown

THE

GUESSING

Who Am I...................

My sweet and saltiness melts in your mouth as you tug and nibble on me, one at a time. Taking me in, depending on your moods. If you want to cry, or laugh, be romanced or in suspense. I can satisfy your cravings until you get what you really want, any time and at any moment during the day.

Who Am I......................

My sweet thickness coats your throat as the steam vaporizers your nostrils with my heavenly scent. Sipping and slurping me slowly with closed eyes rolling in your head. Feeling the heat slide down your chest to the pit of stomach. Warming every crevice of your being until the end.

Who Am I...................

When you pull me, push me, turn me upside down, that turns me on. My body spinning round and round. Sometimes heavy, other times light, depending on how hot you need me to to be to satisfy your need. I will unwrinkle your delectables and lighten your load. Just dial me when you're ready.

Who Am I.................

I relax your body as I soothe your needs. My cream so thick and silky smooth to your touch. Penetrating deeper and deeper with every rub. Moisturizing and massaging into your pores by your strong hands in a circular motion on your spot until your dryness disappears. Leaving your moist and ready.

Who Am I...................

Heating up your skin while at the same time, opening your pores and helping release pent up pressure to ease your body. My hot vapors and pheromones working your senses and putting your mind at ease till daylight. The feeling of pressure draining from your body inch by inch with every breath you take. By dawn I'll have you feeling like a new MAN.

Who Am I....................

You smack me, pop me, and suck me until your jaws get tired, my juices helping to keep your mouth fresh and alive. Savoring my flavors while I'm staying wet and juicy for minutes, sometimes hours on end. So many taste to choose from and yummy beyond your wildest dreams.

Who Am I……………..

As heat touches my brown frame and the water sprinkles shower my mound, you enter me, to explode and expand inch by inch. To burst into your fullest potential and cause the colors of the rainbow to be seen from day into the wonders of night.

Who Am I................

Entering your awaiting space very carefully, while you make sure we meet in the same place perfectly and together. You have measured my length to ensure I'm not too big for your opening so the fit will be tight enough to keep us laced together for the duration of your need.

Who Am I.............

Kneading and caressing me until you lay me flat. Pounding my mound into submission until I'm like dough in your hands. Flipping me as your fingers slowly massage my layers, until I'm spread eagle and waiting to be topped and sprinkled the finest of delectables.

Who Am I................

Teasing me with your stiff tip in a circular motion, switching up between your thickness and full lick of your tongue until your feel me jump. Waiting on the shower of sweetness and as you greedily lap all my juices until dry. Placing your tongue on me until you feel my throbbing, signaling I'm ready for round 2.

Who Am I.....................

Trailing your body from head to toe, creamy, soft and silky. Slipping and sliding through every crack and crevice of your body as I creep down your path of bareness. Sticking to your wetness until sprayed off by Mr. Head.

Who Am I..................

Resting snug between your fat cheeks as they jiggle one pop at a time, curving into a perfect "O" while cuffing and holding your jelly into place as I rise to the occasion. Gripping your hips, not being too obvious and just waiting for the moment when you slide out of me or just leave me altogether.

Who Am I...............

Stroking me in a slow motion, taking your time not missing a spot as I glide across your lips, your awaiting mouth making a perfect pout. I leave my mark until you're moist with my pearly gloss, shaping your fullness as I touch each line and corner, giving your succulent mouth the moisture and ripeness it desires.

Who Am I………………..

As you tighten your strong hands around my roundness to control my body, holding me steady in place. Gripping my sides just right as you maneuver these curves until you reach your desired destination.

Who Am I..................

Bobbing your head up and down with your eyes closed, mouth wide open and hands behind your back, as you go all in, trying to grasp my roundness with the wetness between your lips. "Splashing" while never giving up, with hopes of catching my deliciousness to devour me until you reach my core.

Who Am I...................

Tugging and slobbering on me with your juicy, wet mouth. Going in and out slowly across your gums, rubbing and sucking until feeling the satisfaction you crave as you apply pressure until I break through.

Who Am I.................

Place your sexual desires inside me and and lace me with ribbon. Unwrap and open me wide, slowly, piece by piece until you get your surprise. I can be fragile so please handle me with care. Damaging my insides is a no on cause I can't be replaced or refunded. The prize inside of me is for you only.

Who Am I.....................

You rub my hairy pretty round brown exterior as you use your blade to enter me then slurp down my sweetness into your cocktail of lust. Flakes layering the creaminess of various icings, waiting to be licked and melt in your mouth. The white of my exotic creaminess is often covered with chocolate or sometimes mixed with nut.

Who Am I...................

I can be hard or soft, melting in your mouth as you suck me in and out vigorously. My tanginess becomes invisible on your wet tongue. Sometimes being put inside a tight spot or pickle for you to savor my sweet or sour flavor.

Who I am.................

As the beads of wetness roll down my side, you squirt my juices each time my love button is pushed. My insides cool off your hottest desires in more ways than one. My drip is slow and steady, fluctuating between fast than slow, depending on your need until every drop is gone, quench the fierceness of your thirst.

Who Am I...................

Round and round in a slow or fast pace, you take me to my desired spot. Pushing me to the limit until I can't go any further. My screw game is tight, making me dizzy with your back and forth; never quitting or stopping until I cum to the end of the road.

Who Am I...................

My purring sounds like music to your ears while feeling my smooth vibration near your ass. As you push down on my spot, applying pressure, making me roar louder and louder. Squirting fluids as we float on ultimate journeys, long and hard, until we run out of gas.

Who Am I.................

I send chills up and down your spine and cool your skin while giving you goosebumps at my slightest touch. As you slurp and swallow my hardness, I melt, trickling down your throat. Being cautious not to suck to hard, causing your brain to freeze from my power.

Who Am I.................

Depending on how you can take it creamy or with a lot of hard nuts. My thickness chokes you when you swallow or fill your jaws with too much of me. Pacing yourself, putting me in slowly, with no gagging or assistance from your sweet, jiggly partner. Jamming you both together as I receive pleasure while I smash.

Who Am I.....................

Black, white, or color, size doesn't matter. I can take it all. My results are picture perfect, no flaws, pure perfection. Press my spot to stop. Feed me but don't jam me up!!!

Who Am I...................

The taste of me waters your mouth, anticipating the sting and sharpness you get sucking me in and out, teasing your tip. Inch by inch, one tentative lick at a time, making your eyes leak as you savor my overpowering flavor and you tighten your jaw. Locking your mouth into one place, stuck on sucking me.

Who Am I....................

Turning me on when you put it inside of me, gyrating left to right. Sometimes not jiggling it in the right spot but maneuvering it until it fit just right. My box is wide open for it to enter. Take your time, get it right the first time so I won't lock up and you can't get in it again.

Who Am I.................

As the sweet moans come out of me, causing eargasms, you find yourself searching and searching til you tune in to my hot spot that makes you feel some kind of way.

You carry me with you at all times, feeling my beat every time you touch my round knobs.

Pulses and waves move through your soul when I'm in your ear whispering sweet nothings, making you feel good from the soles of your feet to the the crown of your head. Whatever you need baby, I got it all.

Who Am I..................

My juices rolling down your chin, the anticipation of tasting my sweet nectar has you mesmerized as you inhale the intoxicating scent of my heady aroma. Your hungry mouth slurping me whole, making sure you don't miss a drop of this Georgia fineness.

Who Am I.................

Your eyes light up as you see the tip of my pinkness before you. Your mouth waters and your senses reel, preparing your throat for my gloriousness and the pleasure you are about to receive on this hot, summer's eve. Remaining cautious about getting to the edge of my fruit but enjoying the juiciness of me with no interference.

Who Am I...................

Peeling my layers down slowly, one at a time and it's got you mesmerized at my golden frame. Taking in my firmness at the tip, working your way down while enjoying my fullness in your mouth. Not allowing the excess to deter you from enjoying my split.

Who Am I……………..

You lightly taste me, picking me softly as I melt at the moment the heat of your hot mouth makes contact with my fluffiness. My sweetness making your taste buds go into overdrive; almost putting you in a sugar coma.

Who Am I.................

Intoxicating your soul as I slide down your dry throat, dying to get quenched by my sparkling effervescence. Filled with the richness of the finest textures; swishing through your awaiting cheeks, you swallow me slowly as you enjoy my intoxication.

Who Am I.....................

Lifting my body off my feet making me feel secure as your arms of steel close simultaneously seal the deal. I will reach my destination, pausing only to allow others to enjoy my ride to the "TOP!"

Who Am I………………..

I tantalize your skin with my fluffy texture, caressing you all over. Tickling your hot spots and focusing on pleasing you from head to toe.

My touch is so intimate, especially on your nipples, rotating in a circular motion. Then down the middle between your succulent breast, making my way down to those juicy ass thighs. Mmmm..

Who Am I...................

I can secure you with both arms wrapped tightly around your magnificent body, making you feel comfortable or you can recline in my embrace while I massage your shoulders, down your back, across your ample hips, and pass your plump, curved ass, putting you into a deep, deep slumber.

Who Am I...................

As I suck you in and out my mouth, it's getting wetter and stickier from your sweet, juicy tongue. My goal is to get to the hard center and lick and tug on it until I get to that creamy, explosive middle.

Who Am I...................

When you get blown my way, it heats up my cool skin, causing sweat beads to run down my juicy thighs. Then you trail my body with hot drippings as I moan from the pain and pleasure.

As I cool, he takes his tongue and licks every one of my creative molds from your ultra, sensual skin.

Who Am I……………..

As I traveled up and down your mounds, taking my time, not wanting to miss those voluptuous curves taking me round and round until I reach my final destination.

Oh no… not being in any rush, I'm going in for the long haul and I plan on staying there for a while. It's gets a little bumpy at first, until I get your rhythm then you ride all night until we run out of gas…

A

Little Erotic

Short

___RED EYE___

I was almost in a panic, thinking I was going to miss my flight, choosing a red eye so I wouldn't have to deal with all the hustle and bustle of the crowds.

As I took my seat in the waiting area, I sat across from a fine, chocolate 6'5, 240lb. Hunk of a man. I was trying not to stare but he was real easy on the eyes as I've been told I am. We both sported earplugs, listening our favorite jams. I know this because we both were moving to the beat.

He began rolling his ass in a slow grind while grabbing his dick at the same time, showing a sister what he was working with. I giddily accepted the challenge and spread my thick thighs, giving him a glimpse of my juicy lady. Believe me, I knew what I was working with. I gave him the eye as I strode off to the nearest unisex restroom, knowing he would follow shortly.

Like clockwork, he slowly opened the door, finding me already spread eagle on marble sink top and waiting for his juicy ass lips to go to work.

He licked and sucked on this pussy liked he owned it, pulling on my clit until I squirted my sweet nectar all over his face.

Totally satisfied, I wasn't in the mood to be selfish. I went to my knees, sucking his 9 inch dick like a champ. Before he could cum, he wanted to feel my tightness gripping his big thick pipe. We began tongue kissing, taking each other's breathe as we passionately satisfied one another.

After applying a magnum, he eased those hard 9 inches inside me, filling me to capacity. We fucked each other like it was our last day on earth but being quiet to avoid being interrupted. We climaxed together with pleased smiles, catching our breath in order to compose ourselves. We parted with a peck, knowing this had been a chance of a lifetime and would never be repeated.

He parted first and I exited shortly after as if I was floating on air. We took our seats across from each other, put our earplugs back in, closed our eyes and began listening to our favorite jam but with different looks on our face, not really believing the red eye experience as we passed through the night...

GUESS WHO'S CUMMIN?

THE END

GUESS WHO'S CUMMIN?

AUTHOR CATRINA BROWN

And her brand .CUM

GUESS WHO'S COMING

ANSWERS

I AM MS. KETTLE CORN POPCORN

I AM MS. HOT TEA AND HONEY

I AM MS. DRYER

I AM MR. LOTION

I AM MS. VICK'S VAPOR RUB

I AM MS. CHEWING GUM

I AM MS. SEED AND FLOWER

I AM MR. SHOELACE

GUESS WHO'S CUMMIN?

I AM MS. PIZZA DOUGH

I AM MS. CLIT

I AM MS. SOAP

I AM MS. PANTIES

I AM MR. LIPSTICK

I AM MS. STEERING WHEEL

I AM MS. APPLE & WATER BARREL GAME

I AM MS. PACIFIER AND BABY'S FIRST TOOTH

I AM MS. PACKAGE

I AM MS. COCONUT

I AM MR. NOW & LATER

I AM MS. WATERCOOLER

I AM MS. WHEEL

I AM MR. ENGINE

I AM. MS. ICE CUBE

I AM MR. PEANUT BUTTER AND JELLY

I AM MS. COPY MACHINE

I AM MR. LEMON

I AM MS. KEYHOLE

I AM MS. RADIO

I AM MS. PEACH

I AM MS. WATERMELON

GUESS WHO'S CUMMIN?

I AM MR. BANANA

I AM MS. COTTON CANDY

I AM MS. CHAMPAGNE

I AM MS. ELEVATOR

I AM MR.FEATHER

I AM MR. MASSAGE CHAIR

I AM MS. TOOTSIE POP

I AM MS. FLAME AND CANDLE

I AM MR. TRUCK DRIVER

NOTES

<u>NOTES</u>